the Yes

For M&J,

because yes.

S.B.

First published in Great Britain in 2014 by Andersen Press Ltd., 20 Vauxhall Bridge Road, London SW1V 2SA.

Published in Australia by Random House Australia Pty., Level 3, 100 Pacific Highway, North Sydney, NSW 2060.

Colour separated in Switzerland by Photolitho AG, Zürich.

Printed and bound in Malaysia by Tien Wah Press.

10 9 8 7 6 5 4 3 2 1

British Library Cataloguing in Publication Data available.

ISBN 978 1 84939 710 0 (hardback)

ISBN 978 1 78344 090 0 (paperback)

Sarah Bee   Satoshi Kitamura

the Yes

ANDERSEN PRESS

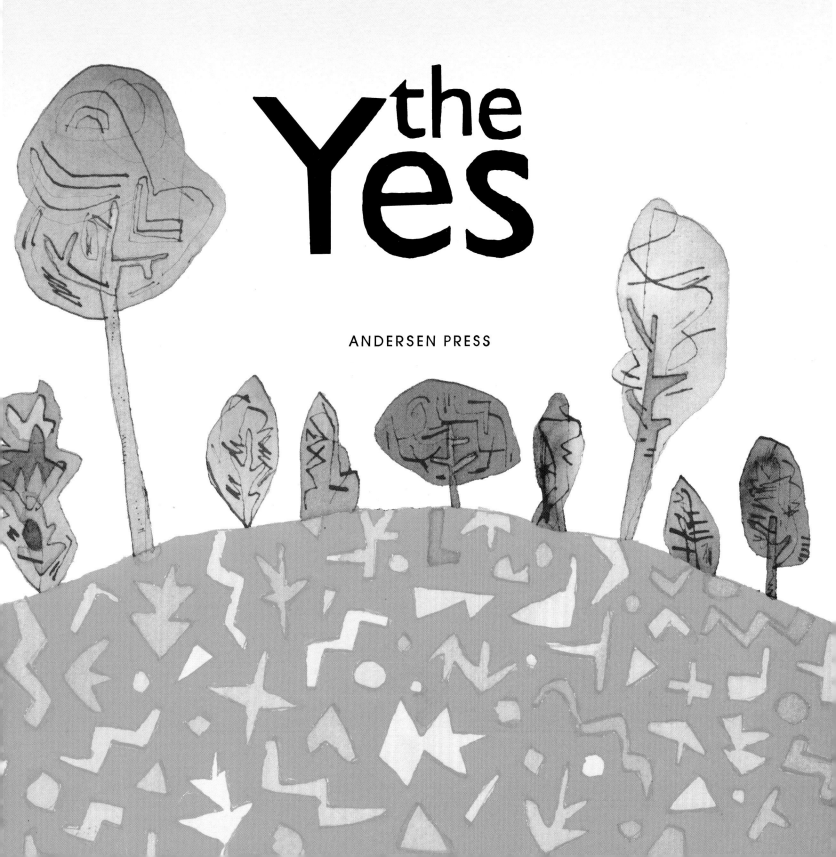

In a soft comfy nest in a safe warm place there
snoozed a great big orange thing called the Yes.
He was snug, but the Yes had a Where to go to.

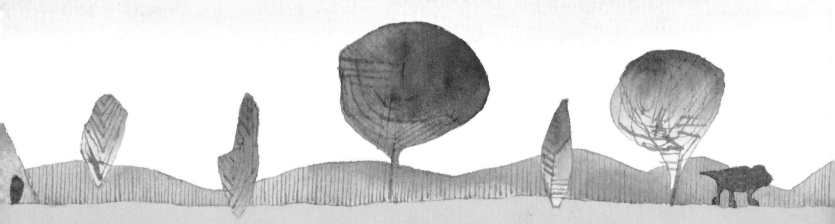

So he left his nest and went trundling out to see.

The Where was an endless place of Nos. The Nos were everywhere and everywhat in swarms and flocks and packs. They teemed and seethed. They picked and nipped and snipped and snicked.

They were so many and so very that you could see nothing but Nos. They made all the Here and all the Else a no-ness and a notness.

The Yes came to a tree. The tree was tall. It had fruit.
The Yes was hungry.

Yes?

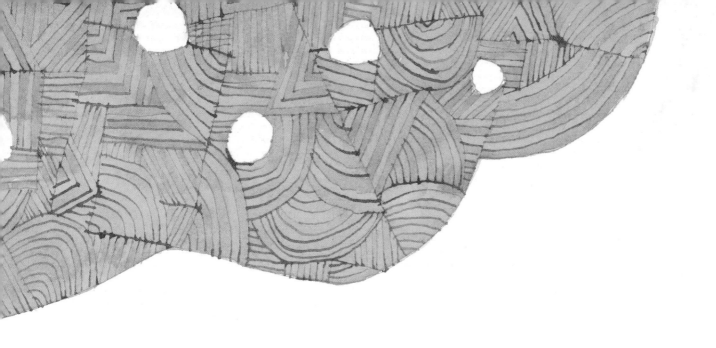

Was the tree too tall to climb?
The Yes was big and lumpen.

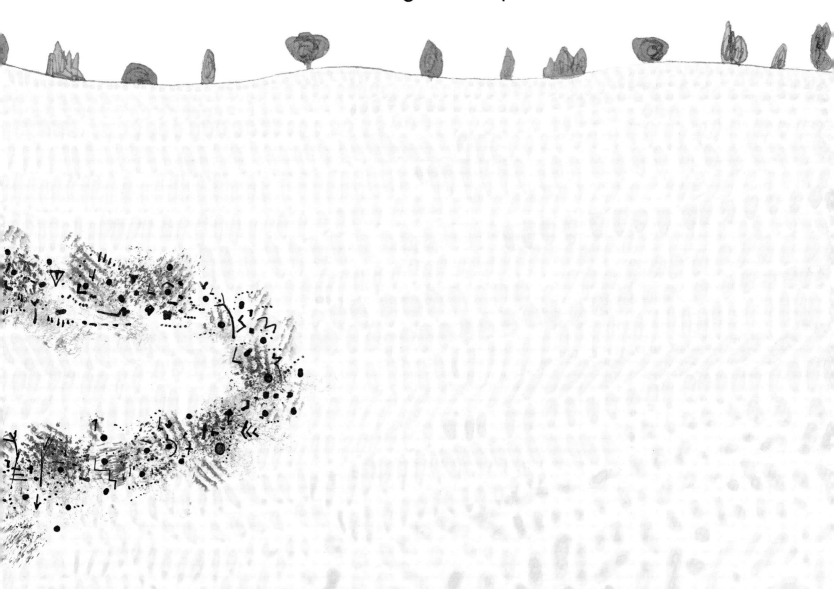

The Nos swarmed around the Yes in a thick cloud
of no and said all the nos there ever were.

"No, too big."

"No, too tall."

"No, too silly."

"No, you'll fall."

NO!

The Nos sat on the Yes and stood on his head and pulled
his ears and tugged his tail. They made such a huge no
you could hear it from the sky and feel it in the ground.

But the Nos were small and the Yes was large. The Nos were flimsy and the Yes was bulky. The Nos were not a thing, and the Yes was a great big thing.

The Yes looked . . .
and climbed the tree.

Yes!

Yes?

The Yes lumbered on.

In a thereish part of the great big Where,
he came to a valley. It had a bridge.
A little flimsy bridge.
The Yes was big and hefty.

Yes?

The Nos came and rained down no all over.

There were Nos in the air, Nos by his feet, Nos in his fur, Nos up his nose.

"NO!" said the Nos.

It is what Nos do and what they are.

"No, you couldn't.

It's too rickety."

"No, you shouldn't.
It's too trickety."

"You will break it.

You won't make it."

NO!

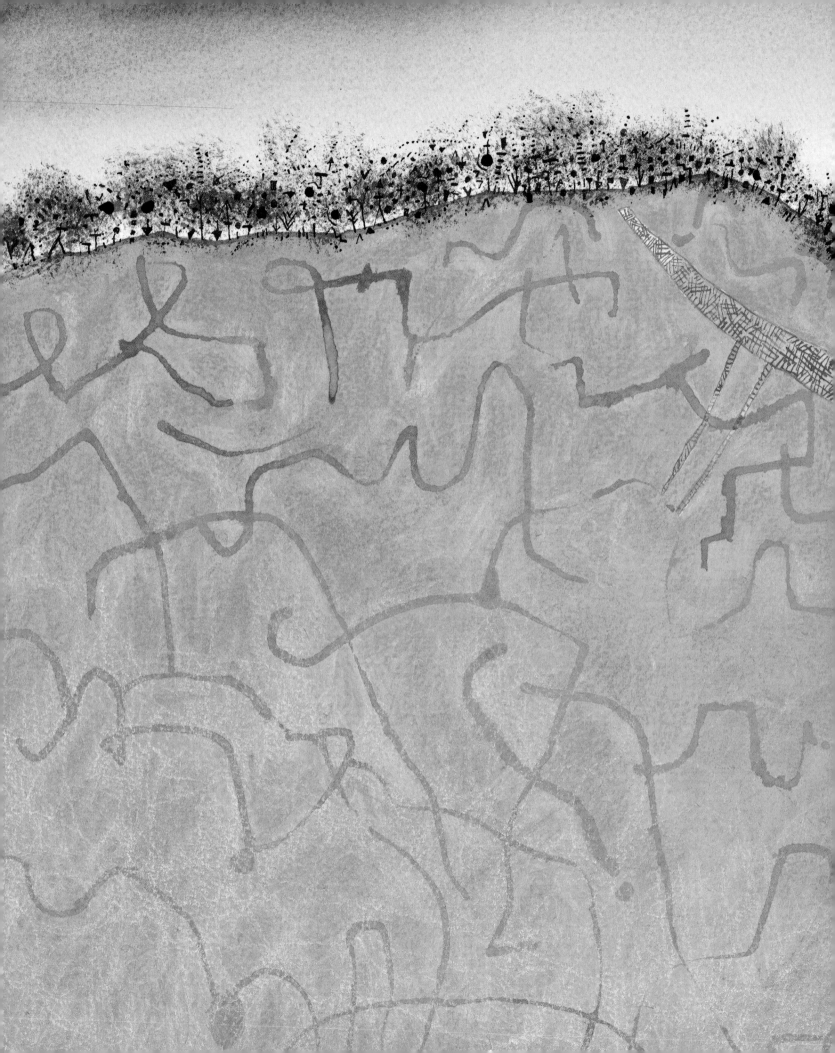

The song of the Nos was loud and long and so full of no there was nothing else to hear.

The Yes looked . . .

Yes!

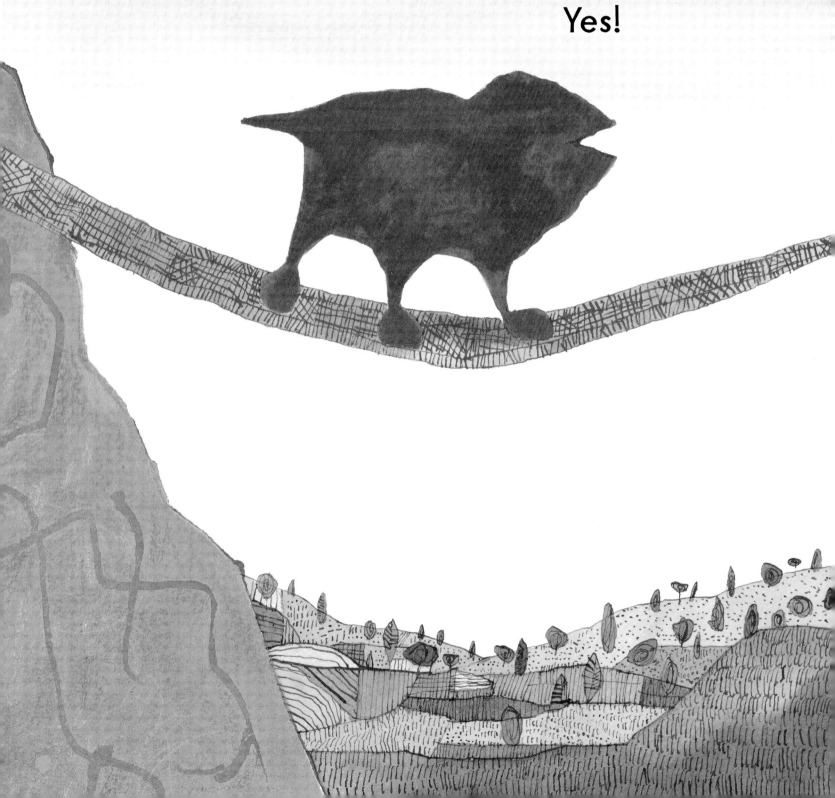

The Yes bumbled on.

In a further part of the big wide Where, he came to a river.

Yes?

"No, no, no, it's much too deep!"

"No, no, no it's far too steep!"

"No, beware!"

"No, don't dare!"

NO!

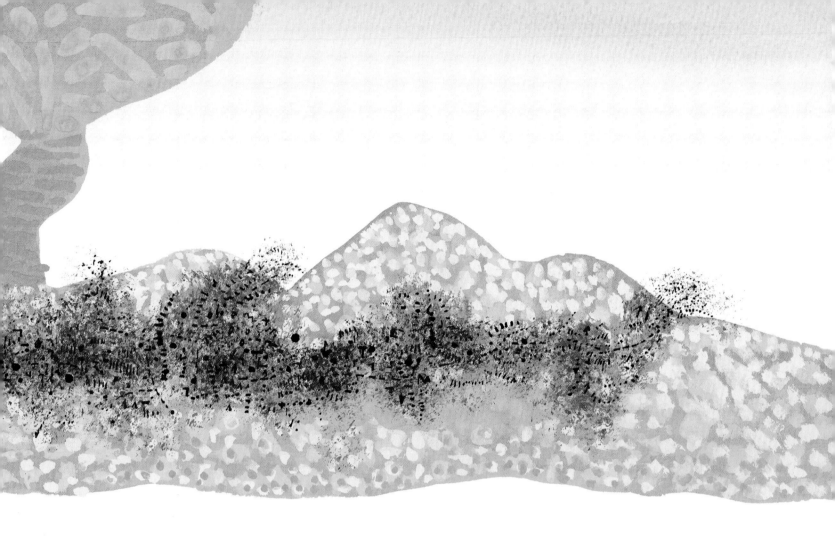

The Nos put up a wall of no that went all
around the Where and into all the This
until everything was full of no.

The Yes looked . . .

Yes!

The Yes gumbled on, and after a When he came to a scary dark wood in the Where.

"No no no no no no no no NO NO NO!"

The Yes rumbled on and on.
He went scrumbling by the marshes and flundering through the fields.

He went over the rocks and bumps and dips, into and out of the wide empty spaces, over and under the bad barren places.

The Nos no-ed and no-ed and no-ed in numbers no one could count.
The Yes only yessed in all his goodness and **bigness** and **yesness**.

And then the Yes came to a big rolling hill. The Nos did the loudest and no-ing-est no they could do. But all the Nos in all the Where all put together were only a no in the end. A no made of dust and nothing, that wasn't ever really there at all.

The Yes went **up,** and **up,**

until the noise of the Nos in their no-ness and notness grew

smaller

and smaller,

and fainter

and fainter,

until there was no more no and never had been.

There was only **the Yes.**

Other wonderful titles illustrated by
Satoshi Kitamura

Angry Arthur
9781842707746

Beetle and Bug
and the Grissel Hunt
9781849396257

Millie's Marvellous Hat
9781842709481

Ned and the Joybaloo
9781842706053

Pot-san's Tabletop Tales
9781849393782